Dwarfie Stane

RETOLD BY JUDY PATERSON

ILLUSTRATED BY SALLY J. COLLINS

KILPATRICK SCHOOL
DALMUIR, CLYDEBANK

THE AMAISING PUBLISHING HOUSE LTD

DEDICATION
For Joyce
They are rich who have true friends

ACKNOWLEDGEMENTS
From the Orkneyinga Saga, the story of the Norse Earls of Orkney
written about 1200 A.D. With thanks to Sheila Maher and
Aileen Paterson for advice and encouragement.

GLOSSARY AND NOTES

Dwarfie   a dwarf
Stane   stone

The original Sigurd was the conniving son of a priest, not the dwarf which is the adaptation of later years under the influence of European folktales. Having previously served in the court of David 1, when he was banished from Orkney he went to the court of Malcolm 1V. Frakokk escaped to her estates in Sutherland and lived to cause further trouble before she was indeed burned in a Viking raid which was planned as revenge. The magic garment of the Orkneyinga Saga was a linen shirt which brought about the death of Harald.

Text © Judy Paterson
Illustrations © Sally J. Collins

Published in 1998 by
The Amaising Publishing House Ltd. Unit 7, Greendykes Industrial Estate,
Broxburn, West Lothian, EH52 6PG, Scotland

Telephone 01506-857570
Fax 01506-858100

ISBN 1 871512 57 3

Printed and bound by Scotprint Ltd, Musselburgh

Page layout by Mark Blackadder

Reprint Code   10   9   8   7   6   5   4   3   2   1

This book is sold subject to the conditions that it shall not, by way of trade or otherwise, be lent, hired out or otherwise circulated without the publisher's prior consent, in any form of binding or cover other than that in which it is published and without a similar condition including this condition being imposed upon the subsequent purchaser.

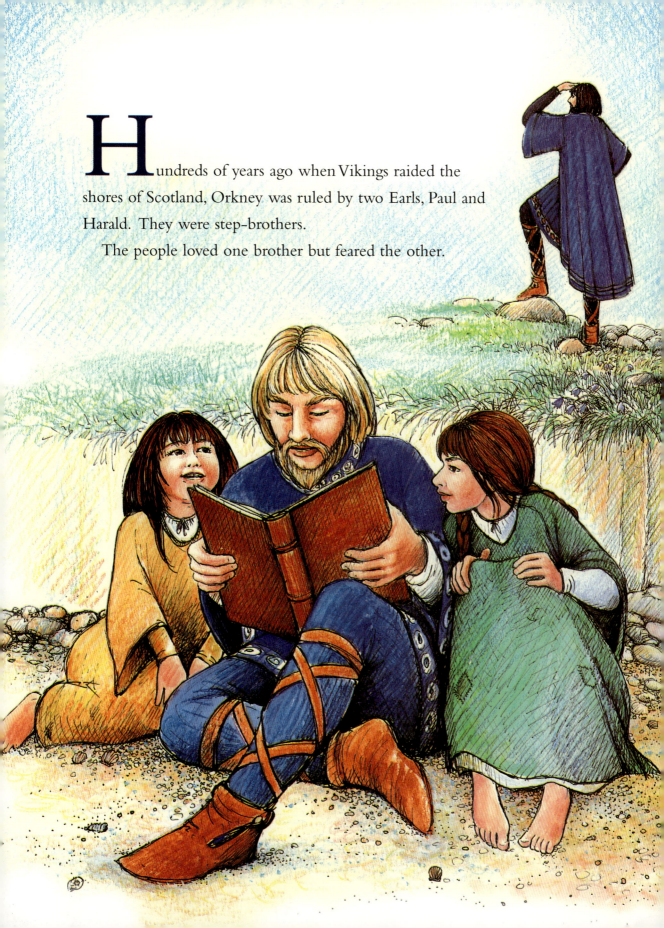

Hundreds of years ago when Vikings raided the shores of Scotland, Orkney was ruled by two Earls, Paul and Harald. They were step-brothers.

The people loved one brother but feared the other.

Paul was a fair-haired, gentle man who was so quiet that people called him Paul the Silent. Harald was dark-haired and so quick with his tongue he was known as Harold Smooth Tongue. But Harold also had a bad temper which was why the people of Orkney were afraid of him. They liked the kindly mannered Paul better.

This made Harold's mother, Helga, very angry.

"There should be only one King of Orkney," she complained to her sister, the Countess Frakokk. "Paul is too soft. Harold is a real leader and he should be King!"

The Countess Frakokk agreed and tapped the side of her nose while she thought what to do.

"I shall travel to the island of Hoy," she murmured with an evil grin. "I shall visit the wizard Sigurd, at the Dwarfie Stane. He may have some magic which will help us."

So Countess Frakokk sailed to the island of Hoy and climbed the steep hill until she reached the Dwarfie Stane. It was a huge slab of sandstone into which two dark chambers had been cut. Long ago it had been a burial place but now it was Sigurd's strange house.

Just then the dwarf appeared with his great black raven.

"I have been waiting for you Countess." he said.

Sigurd was a strange person. He had the body of an ancient twisted old man, as stunted as the wind-swept bushes on the hillside but his face was as young and beautiful as the sun in the early dawn.

"Come inside and tell me how I can help you." Sigurd looked at the Countess with a sly grin. "Perhaps one day you will make me rich and famous."

"Perhaps, if your magic works!" said the Countess, stepping inside.

Meanwhile, Harald had sailed with his mother to visit the King of Scotland who had a grand court where there were many fine things to admire.

"Oh, Harald! What beautiful clothes they wear in Scotland," said Helga.

"What beautiful girls they have in Scotland," said Harald. He was watching a dark-haired girl sitting by the hearth. "I think she would make me a pretty wife. Who is she?"

"That is the Lady Morna from Ireland. She is one of the Queen's attendants," his mother replied. "Go and speak to her."

Harald bowed and kissed Lady Morna's fingertips.

"I am Harald," he announced, "a brave warrior and a great hunter. I am rich and I rule Orkney and all its islands," but he did not tell her about his step-brother, Paul.

The Lady Morna was surprised by Harald's bold speech and replied quietly,

"Power and wealth mean little to me, my Lord."

Over the next
few weeks Harald tried
to impress the Lady
Morna. He boasted
about his castles and
bragged about his
hunting. He
showed her how
skilled he was with
his sword and shield.
Morna was not
interested.

"I wish Harald would leave
me in peace," Morna said to a friend. "He is big-headed
and boring. He is bad tempered and he shouts at the servants."
She sighed, "He is not a very nice man at all."

Then one day Harold asked her to be his wife.

"I cannot marry you. I do not love you," she told him.

Harold was so angry that for once he could not speak. He went in
search of his mother.

"She will not marry me!" he said in disbelief.

"Never mind," said Helga. "She just needs time. I shall speak to the Queen and arrange for Morna to come to Orkney for Christmas. She'll change her mind before the New Year."

The Queen thought Harald would be an ideal husband for her attendant and persuaded Morna to visit Orkney. Poor Lady Morna felt she must do as the Queen wished.

A fter a long voyage, they arrived in Orkney on a cold grey winter's day. Paul was waiting to greet them. He had prepared a great fire and the table was laden with food and wine for the weary travellers.

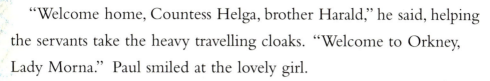

"Welcome home, Countess Helga, brother Harald," he said, helping the servants take the heavy travelling cloaks. "Welcome to Orkney, Lady Morna." Paul smiled at the lovely girl.

"I didn't know Harald had a brother." Morna was surprised. She suddenly felt as if she had found a friend. This quiet man was nothing like his brash brother. "Now I am glad I came to Orkney after all," she smiled.

Harald saw Morna smiling at Paul and he was very jealous.

That night Harald
went to find Paul, who
was busy reading.

"The Lady Morna is to be my wife," announced Harald, clutching
the dagger at his belt.

"I swear I will kill you if you try to take her from me."

Paul closed his book gently and spoke softly to calm his step-brother.

"How could a lady like Morna notice a man as quiet as me, Brother? You have the gift of words and you are known as a brave warrior. I prefer my books and my music to sword-play and dancing. A lady would soon tire of a poor man like me."

Harald's fierce scowl faded away,

"That's the longest speech I have heard from you in years," he exclaimed. "You are right! She will expect to have a good time with feasting, dancing and hunting. She won't be interested in your books and your silent company."

ut Harald was wrong. No matter how he tried to impress the Lady Morna, she was not interested.

"It's a bright frosty morning My Lady, and we are off to hunt otters for sport. Will you come with us?" he asked.

Morna shuddered at the thought,

"I think little of that sport. I shall stay here and read," she said.

Over the next week he asked her to go hawking and riding but she shook her head each time.

Morna spent her days quietly. She did not want to be with the Countess Helga and she was frightened of the Countess Frakokk who watched her all the time. Sometimes she walked with Paul in the garden. Sometimes she listened to Paul playing his harp.

When Harald wanted to dance and drink late into the night, Morna slipped away to her room to dream of Silent Paul.

One morning, Morna saw Paul getting ready for a journey.

"Where are you going?" she asked.

"We celebrate Christmas at the Palace of Orphir. I am going to get things ready," he replied with a sorrowful smile. He did not want to leave Morna because he had fallen in love with her. "You will come with the court in two days time," he sighed, thinking that two days was a long time.

"Let me come now, with you!" the young girl pleaded. "I will not be silent like you Paul. I love you. Do not leave me here alone."

Paul was so happy he put his arms around her and kissed her!

"We shall be married after Christmas," he laughed.

But Morna was frightened and looked over her shoulder in case anyone should hear them,

"Let's keep it a secret. I am afraid of Harald and his aunt, Countess Frakokk," she whispered.

Behind the young couple, a tapestry twitched. Countess Frakokk had seen them. She hissed softly like a snake and slid into the shadows.

"That wedding will not take place," Countess Frakokk muttered angrily. She set out for the Dwarfie Stane immediately.

When she arrived, Sigurd was sitting on the stone slab which had once blocked the entrance of the tomb. She jangled a bag of coins,

"We must find a way to get rid of Paul," she said coldly.

Sigurd shook his head,

"Do not ask me! The people love Paul and they will hunt me down if I help you."

"If you do help me, you will become famous and rich. I will send you to David, the King of Scotland."

The Countess tapped the side of her nose. "Imagine living in a palace, Sigurd."

Sigurd wanted to be rich and famous so he replied softly,

"I will weave a magic cloth with threads of poison. You may cut it and sew it but whoever wears a tunic made of such cloth would surely die."

The Countess laughed wickedly and arranged for the cloth to be sent to the palace.

Not long afterwards, Harald arrived at the Dwarfie Stane.
He was in a really bad mood and he grew even more angry as he
told Sigurd his story.

"I asked the Lady Morna to marry me when I met her in
Scotland but she refused so we brought her back to Orkney. Any
young girl would be pleased to have a brave warrior like me,"
Harald boasted. "But today, just after my brother left for Orphir, I
asked Lady Morna to marry me again, and for the second time
she has refused." He thumped a bag of gold onto the table. "To
make matters worse, she says she loves my brother!"

Sigurd smiled. He searched through his bottles, and gave Harald one full of rosy liquid.

"Pour this into the lady's wine and within twenty-four hours she will love you and forget your brother."

As everyone gathered for supper in
the great hall, Lady Morna felt alone and
frightened. Countess Helga and Countess Frakokk
were watching her. Then she saw Harald pour something into her wine.

When he gave her the goblet she pretended to sip it.

"It's lovely wine Harold," she said with a sweet smile which pleased him greatly.

The cooks brought in dishes of meat and fish and great bowls of hot soup. Each time Harald was busy with his knife or making a joke with friends, Morna tipped some of the wine onto the floor.

Finally Harald noticed the goblet was empty and he wondered if the love potion had worked.

Clever Morna smiled as she offered him a dish of fruit,

"My Lord Earl, I feel very happy tonight." she said. "Tomorrow we shall travel to Orphir and I am so looking forward to Christmas."

Harald was delighted to think that Sigurd's charm had worked but Morna was thinking of Paul who would protect her.

After they arrived at the Palace of Orphir, Harald went hunting while Morna and Paul were happy just being together again.

In a room high at the top of the castle Countess Helga and Countess Frakokk were busy with needles and thread sewing a tunic. They worked upon the most beautiful piece of cloth that shone and sparkled with all the colours of the rainbow. This was the magic cloth from the Dwarfie Stane.

They had just finished the last stitches when Harald burst through the door.

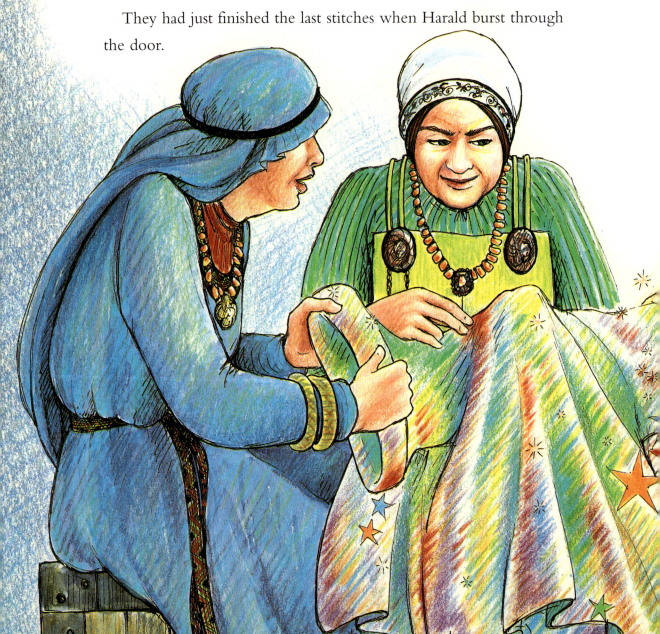

"Sigurd is a fool," he thundered. "His love potion does not work and Morna is in love with Paul. I have just seen them together." Then he saw the shimmering colours of the tunic. "Is this for me?" he said, picking it up.

"It's for Paul," replied Helga, but before she could say anything else, Harald slipped his arm through the sleeve. "Take it off!" she screamed. "It will poison anyone who wears it."

Harald did not listen. "Sigurd's magic does not work. I'll show Paul he cannot have everything," he said as he ran out.

Harald raced down the stairs into the great hall and the two women ran shrieking after him. Then he collapsed onto the floor crying out in pain.

Paul went to help his brother while Helga tried to tear the poisoned tunic off her son.

"Get it off him!" she screeched. "It was not meant for him." But it was too late.

Harald pushed his mother aside and clung to Paul.

"I have wronged you Paul, forgive me." He took a deep breath and gasped, "Beware of those two evil women who want to see you dead."

Harald died in the arms of his step-brother. While the people of the court stood round about deep in shock Helga and Countess Frakokk escaped before anyone noticed.

Silent Paul was very angry.

"They will be punished," he swore. "They will be hunted down and made to pay for this crime. I will go to Hoy and capture Sigurd myself. He shall commit no other wickedness in Orkney!"

But it was not Paul who punished Helga and the Countess. They had escaped to a castle in the north of Scotland and thought they were safe.

One day Viking ships were seen from the castle windows. A fierce band of Viking raiders landed on the beach. In no time at all they had broken down the castle doors. All the gold and silver and jewels were taken and the Vikings set fire to the castle.

Countess Helga and Countess Frakokk died in the flames.

When Paul reached the Island of Hoy, he found the Dwarfie Stane was deserted. There was no sign of Sigurd and none of the Island folk knew where he had gone. Sigurd was never seen again.

To this day, the Dwarfie Stane of Hoy remains an empty and mysterious place . . .